SPACE TAXI

B.U.R.P. STRIKES BACK

By Wendy Mass and Michael Brawer

Illustrated by Keith Frawley

Ⓛ Ⓑ

LITTLE, BROWN AND COMPANY

New York   Boston

Little, Brown and Company

Hachette Book Group
1290 Avenue of the Americas, New York, NY 10104
Visit us at lb-kids.com

Little, Brown and Company is a division of Hachette Book Group, Inc.
The Little, Brown name and logo are trademarks of Hachette Book Group, Inc.

The publisher is not responsible for websites (or their content) that are not owned by the publisher.

First Edition: January 2017

Library of Congress Cataloging-in-Publication Data
Names: Mass, Wendy, 1967– author. | Brawer, Michael, author. | Frawley, Keith, illustrator.
Title: B.U.R.P. strikes back / by Wendy Mass and Michael Brawer ; illustrations by Keith Frawley ; based on the art of Elise Gravel.
Description: First edition. | New York ; Boston : Little, Brown and Company, 2017. | Series: Space taxi ; 5 | Summary: "Eight-year-old Archie Morningstar, his father, and the talking cat Pockets travel to Akbar's Floating Rest Stop, where Pockets is going to receive an award for bravery. But when all the tuna fish (Pockets' favorite food) goes missing, they must discover who is behind the nefarious plot." —Provided by publisher.
Identifiers: LCCN 2015049771| ISBN 9780316308410 (hardback) | ISBN 9780316308403 (trade paperback) | ISBN 9780316308380 (ebook)
Subjects: | CYAC: Interplanetary voyages—Fiction. | Adventure and adventurers—Fiction. | Fathers and sons—Fiction. | Science fiction. | BISAC: JUVENILE FICTION / Science Fiction. | JUVENILE FICTION / Science & Technology. | JUVENILE FICTION / Action & Adventure / General. | JUVENILE FICTION / Animals / Cats.
Classification: LCC PZ7.M42355 Bur 2017 | DDC [Fic]—dc23
LC record available at https://lccn.loc.gov/2015049771

HC: 10 9 8 7 6 5 4 3 2 1
PB: 10 9 8 7 6 5 4 3 2 1

LSC-C

Printed in the United States of America

For our parents.
—WM and MB

For Mom and Dad. Love you
both to the moon and back.
—KF

CONTENTS

Chapter One:

Chapter Two:

Chapter Three:

Chapter Four:

Chapter One:
Pockets Gets Big News

When you live with a talking alien cat, life gets pretty weird. Pockets—whose real name is Pilarbing Fangorious Catapolitus—is a very important agent of the International Security Force, or the ISF for short. It's been two weeks since my dad's space taxi brought us back home after capturing the *Galactic*, the huge spaceship owned by the universe's most dangerous criminal organization, B.U.R.P. In this time, my little sister, Penny, has forced Pockets to participate in many embarrassing situations:

1. She invited him to a tea party with her stuffed dragon, a bear, and an old doll missing both arms. Pockets didn't want to be rude, so he lapped at the tea, but it turned out the tea was not actually tea at all, but rather brown Play-Doh mixed with warm water. This led to many hurried trips to the litter box.

2. Then she held a make-believe wedding between Pockets and Penny's armless doll. Penny put the doll in a dress and tied Dad's best bow tie around Pockets' neck. She made me act as the ring bearer, and I had to walk down the hallway carrying two gold rings (crafted out of yellow Play-Doh, which Pockets now knew better than to eat) on a pillow. Later, when I jokingly referred to the doll as "Pockets' wife," he took a swipe at me with one sharp claw and left a scratch that required a Band-Aid and a formal apology, which he only gave grudgingly.

3. When Penny saw the wound, she immediately decided Pockets must be too riled up and needed a spa treatment to relax. So she gave him a body massage, which I think he actually enjoyed, because he fell asleep in the middle of it. When I pointed that out to him later, he claimed that he

hadn't fallen asleep at all, but rather had passed out from the embarrassment of getting a massage from a little girl while a clay mask dried on his face and warm booties heated his paws. I'm not so sure.

Tonight I have been instructed to tell Penny that Pockets is taking a post-dinner nap so that she can't test out her new purple hair powder on him. Instead of sleeping, though, he's currently in my closet getting the latest report from the ISF on what they've discovered by searching B.U.R.P.'s spaceship.

Even though Sebastian—the head of B.U.R.P.—escaped with plenty of secrets, the ship has been turning up lots of great information. Unfortunately, Pockets said it's "classified," which means it's top secret and "better for my safety if I don't know."

"Wait, what?" Pockets suddenly shouts, flying out of the closet. He skids on four paws across my room, coming to a halt at my feet. He lifts one paw to his mouth and speaks into his watch. "I have to make a speech? Are you sure? Can't I just say thank you and then we eat tuna sandwiches?"

The voice coming through the watch sounds both breathless and excited. "No, my excellent leader. Your fans will have come from near and far to bask in your wondrous presence. They will want to hear from you."

Pockets must have hung up with the ISF already, because that voice could only belong to Feemus, the head (and I'm pretty sure the founder and maybe the only member) of Pockets' fan club. Sure, my family and I think Pockets is awesome, and are super-impressed with his bravery, intelligence, and skill, but Feemus takes his adoration to a whole other level. Pockets can barely stand to be around the little red one-eyed alien, which might seem mean, but I think he's embarrassed by all the attention.

A few months ago, I wouldn't have thought it was possible for a cat to get embarrassed. But a few months ago I didn't know there were such things as aliens or flying taxis that could take you to any planet in the universe. I certainly never guessed I'd meet a talking cat who worked for the ISF and helped keep the universe safe! Or that this cat would invite me and Dad to work with him, or that he'd come to live in my house! It's been a crazy time, but I love it, and so does Dad. I'm not sure how Mom feels having half her family flying around in outer space all the time, but she's a good sport about it, usually.

At only four years old, Penny still thinks Dad drives a regular taxi and that Pockets is a regular cat. Until she learns how to keep secrets, that's the way it has to be, especially now that's she's finally started talking!

"Let's see what my father has to say about this," Pockets says, then angrily hits his watch with his opposite paw to disconnect the call.

"What's going on?" I ask.

"Feemus said I'm getting a big award on Akbar's Floating Rest Stop this weekend and I'm supposed to give a speech. Ugh!" Pockets begins pacing in circles. I glance down at the rug. His claws are cutting a perfect circle into the cloth. I've never seen him this worked up, so I feel it's best not to mention that Mom is very fond of this rug and he'll have to answer to her when she discovers it's been ripped to shreds.

"An award sounds like a *good* thing," I point out. "You told me you've gotten plenty of medals before. Why are you so upset about this one?"

Instead of answering, he whips out his tablet and calls his father. "Hello, son!" the ISF chief shouts. "How's life on Earth?"

"We need to talk," Pockets declares.

I lean over to wave at the screen. "Hi, Chief, how ya doing?"

He gives me a salute. "Fine, Archie boy. It's a lovely day here on Friskopolus!"

Pockets stops pacing and glares at

the screen. "You're in a particularly good mood," he says, clearly suspicious. "What gives?"

His father grins, which makes his long white whiskers quiver. "It's not every day one learns his son is going to be awarded the ISF's highest prize for bravery."

"So they're giving it to me for capturing B.U.R.P.'s most important spaceship and finally identifying its leader, something no other agent had been able to do?" Pockets asks.

"Well, no," his father says, shifting in his chair, "not exactly. Actually, the award is for being the only cat willing to go to the planet Canis."

"But I didn't even go on the ground," Pockets argues. "You know that."

The chief leans back. "This award is quite the honor for us both, don't you think?" he asks, as though he didn't hear Pockets at all. "And it's a big deal for all the agents stationed on Friskopolus who assisted you at the end of the mission."

Pockets opens his mouth to argue, but his anger must have deflated in the face of his dad's enthusiasm. "I guess it was brave. But is it really necessary to make such a big deal about it?"

"The ceremony is excellent publicity for the entire ISF," his father says. "For such a famous place as Akbar's Floating Rest Stop to be hosting it in their brand-new ballroom, well, that will remind all the criminals out there that we are a force to be reckoned with, yes indeed."

Pockets' shoulders slump. "But do I really need to give a speech?"

"You'll do great," his father assures him. "Just pretend only your closest friends and family will be listening instead of a few hundred important guests and anyone tuning in on a remote device. So really, no more than a few million listeners. I'd say ten mil, tops."

Pockets drops the tablet and makes no move to pick it up. I bend down for it. "Pockets seems a bit shocked right now," I tell the chief. "Anything I can do to help him prepare?"

"That is a kind offer," he replies. "The ISF is well aware of the roles you and your father played in the mission. You will both be our honored guests at the ceremony on Sunday. We will put you up in Akbar's finest hotel room, and all your food for the weekend will be on us. Bring your nicest outfit. It will be a very fancy affair."

"Wow, thanks! I'm, um, not sure I have the right clothes, though. And I've never seen my dad in a suit."

"Never mind that, then," he says. "Akbar's personal tailor has been hired to fit Pockets for a suit. I will have him tend to you and your father as well."

At the mention of a suit, Pockets scampers under the bed.

"I'd better go," I tell the chief. "I might need to find some cat treats to get Pockets into the taxi."

"Make sure you check in to the hotel tomorrow by nine to get your itinerary. This will tell Pockets what time he is expected to be at each activity. It will be a

13

very busy day, with fittings, tours, rehearsals, and more, so make sure you get plenty of rest. The award ceremony will be held the following day at a special lunch."

"Yes, sir."

"And please remind my son that his speech should thank all the agents he's ever worked with, and—"

At the word *speech*, Pockets began to whimper. It is very distracting.

"I'm sorry, sir," I say, reluctantly cutting him off. "I'd really better go."

"Remember, the first suit fitting is at ten sharp," the chief says. "Don't be late." The screen goes blank.

I kneel down and peer under the bed. "You coming out?"

Pockets shakes his head.

"Come on, it won't be that bad. It's always fun going to Akbar's. Your favorite Barney's Bagels and Schmear is there. And we'll get to see our friends Graff and Bloppy again!"

Pockets doesn't answer.

"Fine." I sigh. "I'll go get you some cat treats, but after that you'll have to start working on your speech."

Getting him to come out takes a full bag of treats and the reminder that if he doesn't want to write his speech, I could always have Penny give him a bubble bath. The fact that he actually pauses to consider that option tells me how much he REALLY doesn't want to give a big speech. I'm already in pajamas by the time he finally pulls out a notebook and pencil.

With Mom's help, it doesn't take long to pack my suitcase. I'm really excited about the trip. Since the capture of the B.U.R.P. ship, all the criminals in the universe must be lying low, because we haven't been called on any missions recently. I've gone to work with Dad, shuttling aliens between planets as usual, which is awesome, but not always very exciting.

I climb into bed and watch as Pockets rips page after page out of his notebook and crumples them up. "Um, feel free to do that in the closet," I suggest, yawning. "Or, you know, anywhere else at all." But Pockets ignores me. He continues scratching on the paper, grunting, ripping, and crumpling ALL NIGHT LONG. Didn't he hear his dad say we should get a good night's sleep?

I finally wind up carrying my blanket into Penny's room. When I curl up at the foot of her bed, she murmurs, "That's a good Pockets," and scratches me behind the ear before flopping back down to sleep.

Pockets owes me big-time for this.

Chapter Two:
Off to Akbar's

I wake up to find that Penny has tucked her stuffed dragon under my arm and stuck four different butterfly-shaped hair clips in my hair. This is one of those moments when I wish I had a little brother instead of a little sister. I pull the clips out, taking chunks of hair with them, and stumble across the hall to my room. It feels like I only slept an hour.

"That's a good look for you," Dad says from behind me. I turn to see him coming from the kitchen with an egg burrito in his hand. He gestures to my hair, which I know is sticking up in many different directions. I try to smooth it down but doubt it does much good.

"I wish you could come," I say to Mom as she piles pancakes onto my plate. "You wouldn't believe all the different aliens that come and go at Akbar's."

"I think I'm better off with both feet on Earth," Mom says. "And you don't think Bubba—the guy who lived under the sink for a while—was the only alien your father ever brought home, do you? Remind me to tell you about the others someday."

"I will!" I say, my mouth full of pancake.

"Make sure you mind your manners at the fancy lunch," Mom warns. "That means no talking with your mouth full. Put your napkin on your lap and use it—no wiping your mouth on your sleeve. Say *please* and *thank you*. And if you don't like something you're served, just say *no thank you* instead of pushing it away and saying *gross*."

I nod, although honestly, I'm so drowsy I know I'm going to forget all that before I even finish breakfast. I'm sure I'll find some way to embarrass myself when I get there. At least we don't have to leave before dawn anymore. Pockets gave the airfield a lifetime supply of Camo-It-Now, and all the space taxis get sprayed to look like regular planes as we pull in.

Mom and Penny watch from the porch as Dad and I climb into the taxi. Pockets is already in the backseat, checking his messages. He puts his tablet on the seat when Penny runs down the steps and up to his window. I'm wondering if she's going to ask why the cat needs to come with us—which really is a valid question. Instead, she sticks her little arm in and places a small item on Pockets' head. "For luck," she explains.

Pockets tilts his head forward in a very *I'm just a regular cat*–like gesture, and the object falls to the seat. I reach over the back of my seat for it and hold it up so Dad and Pockets can see. It's a green plastic four-leaf clover.

"From my cereal box!" Penny says proudly.

"That's a lovely gift," Mom says, swooping her up. They wave as we drive away. As soon as we get down the street, Pockets snatches the clover from my hand. "Mine," he says, and slips it into one of his pockets so quickly I don't even see it leave his paw.

"Sheesh," I say, turning back around. "Someone's crabby this morning."

"Sorry," he grumbles. "I didn't get much sleep."

"Join the club!" I reply.

"Why didn't *you* sleep?" he asks.

He truly seems not to know that he kept me up! Before I can tell him, he says, "Never mind. Too tired to chitchat. Wake me when we get there."

"Wait—did you finish your speech, Pockets?" my dad asks as the taxi turns in to the airfield.

I'm pretty sure Pockets is still awake, because I don't hear snoring yet, but he ignores Dad's question. Dad sighs. "I'll take that as a no."

"Off for a little vacation, Morningstar?" Minerva's squeaky voice comes through the com line. She's usually the one to coordinate Dad's flights for his regular taxi job. Somehow she keeps track of where every alien is going and when they need to be there. Her job is very stressful, apparently.

"As a matter of fact, yes, we *are* going on vacation," Dad says cheerfully.

"Saving the universe all the time must be tiring," she says. I can almost see her eyes rolling from here. If a mouse's eyes CAN roll, that is! Minerva isn't a big fan of Pockets, so she isn't very impressed with my dad's other job, using the space taxi to help solve crimes.

"Actually," I pipe up, "Pockets is getting a big award tomorrow. We're all going to cheer him on. Maybe you can come."

Silence. "Yeah, that wouldn't really work for me," she says. Then she snaps back to business mode and says, "You are third in line for takeoff. Await my orders."

Dad mutes our end of the com line and chuckles. "Can you imagine Minerva at a lunch full of hungry cats?"

I shake my head. "Guess it wouldn't be the best place for a mouse. I'd like to meet her one day, though."

"Me, too," Dad says.

"You've never met her?" I ask in surprise.

He shakes his head. "She and your grandfather were close, but I've never met her. She's stationed on a satellite in Earth's orbit. Maybe one day we'll drop by."

"Pull onto the runway, Morningstar," Minerva squeaks.

Dad un-mutes the com line. "Yes, ma'am. Over and out."

It's rare that I get to see other space taxis as they lift off, so even though my eyes keep trying to close, I watch until they are swallowed up by the clouds. When it's our turn, the rumbling and vibration of the engine are enough to keep my attention, but once we're up off the ground, it's a struggle to stay awake. My arms and legs just feel so heavy. Dad doesn't need my guidance until we're out of the solar system, so I leave my map open on my lap and lean my head back for just a second.

"Archie!" Dad shouts. "I need directions!"

My eyes fly open. Heart pounding, I look up at the darkness of space and then quickly down at the map. "To Akbar's!"

I scream at it. Planets and star systems between our current location and Akbar's pop up into the air. Is that still Earth? I must have the map upside down!

Dad swerves to avoid something and Pockets flies up to the roof and back down. I frantically look at the map to see what we almost hit. Oh, no! I was wrong about him not needing guidance in our own solar system. That was the International Space Station! There are people LIVING there! What if they saw us?

Also, Pockets should really tighten his seat belt!

My map readjusts as Dad turns and steps on the gas, hard. "Turn left at the triple star system," I tell him, gripping the arms of my seat as he corrects his path.

When we're back on track, I gulp and say, "I'm really sorry about that, Dad." I feel awful for letting him down. My mistake could have caused a serious accident.

"Just try to stay awake from this point on," he says.

"You don't have to worry about that," I promise. "That sure woke me up! Do you think anyone on the International Space Station spotted us?"

He shook his head. "Our speed is much too fast to be picked up by their technology."

Relieved that I didn't just blow our cover, I focus carefully on the map the rest of the way. The flashing neon signs that reach high above Akbar's welcome us as we make our final approach. The lights are so festive, like a nonstop party in the otherwise dark sky. Not for the first time, I wish Penny could see this. She'd love it.

Dad steers the taxi around toward the far side of the huge floating building, a part of the rest stop I've never seen. Giant floating letters announce: HOTEL GUESTS ONLY! IF YOU DON'T HAVE A RESERVATION, KEEP ON DRIVING! THIS MEANS YOU! Each letter is bigger than our taxi!

Dad drives right through the center of the *o* in *Hotel* and I realize we're now inside a tunnel. It's so dark that I can't even tell where the sides are. "It's as dark as a wormhole in here!" I say.

"That won't last long," Dad assures me. He's right. A few seconds later light explodes all around us and the taxi fills with loud rock music! Pockets screeches and hits the ceiling again. He covers his ears. The music abruptly cuts off and a deep yet pleasant voice says, "Greetings, honored guests! A transport bot will meet your car shortly to escort you and your luggage to your rooms. Have a lovely visit, and do let us know if we can do anything to make your stay more pleasant!"

"You can have better taste in music," Pockets mumbles.

The taxi comes to a halt in front of a pair of huge glass doors. A woman with her hair braided in an elaborate design on the top of her head opens my door. "Welcome, young Morningstar. I am your bellwoman. I shall be showing you, your father, and Pilarbing Fangorious to your rooms. I am certain you will find them to your liking."

Trying to remember my manners, I reply, "Thank you, I'm sure it will be—" But when I look up, the words get caught in my throat. I've seen some strange things in my role as an ISF deputy—creatures of all shapes, sizes, and colors, with varying amounts of limbs, eyes, and even heads. But never before have I seen anything like the woman—I mean transport bot— holding my car door open.

CHAPTER THREE:
Hotel in the Air

The transport bot looks like a normal person from the waist up, but from the waist down she is a golf cart. Yes, a GOLF CART. Like a little electric cart that you'd drive around in, with space in the back for golf clubs, or in this case, our suitcases.

The transport bot doesn't seem to notice my reaction. Her arms extend superlong, and she cheerfully lifts our suitcases out of the trunk and places them in the cart. SO WEIRD. Pockets barely gives the bot a second look, but Dad raises one eyebrow as he shakes her hand.

We follow her into the hotel lobby, where she instructs us to take seats in the cart. Dad and I exchange a look, but we climb in after Pockets. The lobby is very fancy, with black-and-white-tiled floors and art-work on every wall. Plush couches are full of aliens from all over, everyone dressed in their finest. Dad and I are definitely under-dressed in our jeans and T-shirts!

We drive toward the glass elevator and pull in beside a male transport bot with stacks of pillows and towels in his cart.

The two bots nod pleasantly at each other. The elevator only stops once, to let on a tall man with bumpy blue skin carrying two huge buckets of ice. At first I think he's going to bonk his head on the ceiling, but then the ceiling raises up a few inches, like our taxi does when it turns into a plane. He fits! Very cool. I enjoy looking out the glass walls at the bustling lobby as the elevator slowly rises.

When the door opens at our floor I spot Feemus, pacing up and down the hall, checking his watch. Feemus is so small that at first the bot doesn't even notice him and almost runs him down. Feemus scoots out of the way just in time.

"Finally!" he shouts with joy. Then he hops right into the cart! His one eye beams happily at us.

Pockets groans and slaps his head. "Guess I should have known you'd be here." The tall blue guy gives Feemus a long look as the elevator door closes. Bet he's never seen a little red alien with one eye so excited to see a giant cat!

"I will take it from here," Feemus tells the bot, tossing out the suitcases like they weigh nothing at all. The transport bot hands Feemus a large brown envelope before nodding at us and gliding back to the elevator.

Feemus keeps up a running one-sided conversation as he leads us down a long carpeted hallway that smells like fruit, for some reason. Pockets hurries ahead toward the room.

"Wait," Feemus calls after him. "Don't you want this?" He pulls a typewritten sheet of paper out of the envelope, but

Pockets keeps walking. Dad leans over and takes it. "Sorry about Pockets. It's nothing personal."

"Oh no," Feemus says, "Pockets can act any way he likes. He's earned it!"

I'm sure my mom would scold Pockets for his lack of manners, but it doesn't look like Feemus ever will.

"That is your itinerary," Feemus explains to Dad. He hands me my own copy, which makes me feel grown-up. We catch up to Pockets at the end of the hall.

"Please look it over and let me know if you have any questions." He glances at Pockets. "As always, your comfort is my highest priority."

I scan the page of text. Wow, Feemus wasn't kidding—we have somewhere to be every second, starting in ten minutes!

10:00 a.m. Pockets and the Morningstars will meet with the tailor, who will be taking their measurements.

11:30 a.m. Pockets will present a golden wrench to Kurf (Graff's son), honoring him as the newest mechanic at Graff's Garage.

12:30 p.m. Lunch with important leaders from other planets.

2:00 p.m. Back to the tailor to try on the clothes.

3:00 p.m. A two-hour guided tour of the Akbar Gardens, voted one of the top ten best gardens across ten galaxies.

5:00 p.m. Pockets will judge the slog-eating contest.

6:00 p.m. Dress rehearsal for Sunday's luncheon, followed by a private dinner with Pockets, his fan club, the Morningstars, Pockets' father, and Akbar.

"Akbar himself?" I ask, looking up from the page.

Feemus nods, jumping from foot to foot. "A big honor, yes, indeed!" He finally stops in front of a door and I can't help thinking that the transport bot could have gotten us here a lot quicker. The metal plate on the door tells us we're in the Presidential Suite. Sounds fancy already!

"You will all be sharing these rooms," he tells us. "But Pockets gets the biggest bedroom." He holds the card key up to the metal plate and the door swings open.

Well, the fruit smell is no longer a mystery. Every surface is covered with gift baskets and bowls of exotic fruits from all over the universe! The room itself is huge, reminding me a little of the head of B.U.R.P.'s private rooms on the *Galactic*, but without the criminal mastermind sleeping in one of the beds. I run inside and duck my head into the three bedrooms that branch off from the main living room. Yup, beds are all clear!

"You will find a coupon book on the desk with discounts for various shops and restaurants, even *Barney's*!" Feemus beams.

Pockets' ears twitch at the name of his favorite restaurant.

"But you won't even need to go there," Feemus says excitedly, "because I made

41

sure the main course for lunch tomorrow is Barney's tuna sandwiches!"

Even though this news must make Pockets very happy, he doesn't show it. I notice he has a hard time thanking Feemus for anything. Dad elbows Pockets, who finally mutters, "Thank you." Feemus beams at the small gesture of appreciation.

"If you are ready," Feemus says from the hall, "I will now escort you to the tailor for your fittings."

Dad and I are too busy shoveling what looks like a combination of blueberry and watermelon into our mouths to answer.

"And I can't WAIT to hear your speech!" Feemus gushes. "I bet it's CHOCK-FULL of wisdom and guidance. Perhaps you will share it with me as we walk?"

In response, Pockets growls, "We'll meet you there." Then he springs toward the door and slams it shut.

Dad and I shake our heads. Poor Feemus. He doesn't stand a chance.

Chapter Four:
Archie Makes a Friend

Pockets has locked himself in the huge bathroom to try to write his speech. Dad and I keep telling him through the door that we have to go to the tailor now. Dad's usually calm voice has taken on an edge of frustration. "Pockets, if we're late for the very first thing on our agenda, the whole schedule will get out of whack. Just write what's in your heart."

Pockets only whimpers in response. Dad leans against the door. "Look, I know you don't like being the center of attention. You just want to do your job. And you may not feel like you were particularly brave on the dog planet, but no other cat has even *gone* there. So here we are in this beautiful hotel, with lots of people who came to celebrate you, and you need to try to make the best of it. Or, as my father used to say when faced with something he didn't want to do: *If you can't get out of it, get into it!*"

"Grandpa said that?" I ask.

Dad nods. "Pretty wise, your grandfather."

The door to the bathroom slowly opens. Pockets squares his shoulders. "You're right. Let's do this!" He shoves his notebook deep into a front pocket, grabs a pawful of fruit, and marches out the door. Dad and I hurry after him.

In an effort to keep up his new positive attitude, Pockets greets everyone we pass, holds open doors for the young and old, and picks up two pieces of trash. It is inspiring to watch.

I try not to fall too far behind as we make our way through the hotel lobby, but my attention keeps getting pulled away by places like Hair Today, Gone Tomorrow. All kinds of aliens—some with hair down to their toes—sit in rows facing full-length mirrors and chatting with three-armed robot barbers who snip and spray and blow-dry, all at the same time!

Once we leave the hotel lobby, Dad pulls out the itinerary and studies the map attached to it. He and Pockets both know their way around Akbar's, but neither of them has visited the tailor before.

"Looks like the tailor is all the way on the other end of the rest stop," Dad says, frowning. "It's a few doors down from the roller rink."

"We can visit Bloppy!" I exclaim.

"Feemus will self-destruct if we make any detours now," Dad says. "We'll see Bloppy later."

Dad tries to hold on to Pockets by the scruff of his neck when we pass Barney's, but it's no good. He breaks free easily and runs in. Dad and I reach the counter in time to hear Pockets shout, "What do you mean there's no tuna?"

"All our tuna is being made into sandwiches for the big luncheon tomorrow," the clerk tells him. "Some famous ISF officer is being honored. It's a pretty big deal, I guess."

"That's me!" Pockets cries. "*I'm* the famous ISF officer! And I don't want to wait until lunch tomorrow for my tuna!"

"*You're* the officer?" the clerk says. "I don't think so." He stretches his neck so he can see around Pockets. "Next on line?" It's the blue bumpy guy, asking to buy ice. The clerk shakes his head. "Out of ice. Next!" Boy, people are striking out left and right at Barney's today.

It takes both Dad and me using all our

strength to yank Pockets away from the counter and drag him out. He keeps shouting, "I want to speak to Barney! Get me Barney!"

So much for his new positive attitude.

Feemus throws up his hands when we finally arrive at the tailor's, a half hour behind schedule. "You're here, you're finally here!"

"Let's get this over with," Pockets says, barreling his way into the shop.

"Sorry we're late," Dad tells Feemus. "Pockets had a few meltdowns. He's having trouble with his speech, and then he found out Barney's is out of tuna, and, well, you know how he is."

Feemus nods knowingly. "I certainly *do* know how he is," he says. "It is terribly hard to be as perfect as Pockets all the time. How very lucky you are to always bask in his presence."

"Sure," Dad says. "Lucky. That's us!"

An alien who looks like a cross between a snake and, well, a snake with shoes approaches us. "Come, gentlemen," he says in a slithery voice. "We have been expecting you."

We follow him to the middle of the store and find Pockets standing on a round platform while another snake-alien wraps his tail around Pockets' belly. The snake then whips his tail away and examines it. There's a tape measure printed on his tail! When he's done, he uses the tip of his tail to punch the measurements into a computer.

Dad and I each climb up onto our own

raised platforms, and between the two snakes, they curl their tails around our legs, arms, necks, hips, and waists. It tickles and I have to bite my lip to keep from laughing. "Excuse me for asking," Dad says hesitantly, "but how do you sew the clothes? I mean, without hands?"

The two snake-aliens laugh. "Very carefully!" one of them replies, sticking a sewing needle between his teeth.

"All done," the other says with a final flick of his tail. "Come back at two."

Feemus ushers us out of the tailor's. "No time to waste," he says. "We only have five minutes to get to Graff's Garage."

I glance longingly at the roller rink, ablaze with lights and music. I know my visit to Bloppy will have to wait. At least

I'll get to see Graff and meet his son. I didn't even know he *had* a son!

Feemus tries to talk to Pockets as we walk but eventually gives up when Pockets doesn't look up from his notebook. Hopefully he'll feel better when he finishes writing that speech.

"Sal Morningstar, you old dog!" Graff says, greeting us at the entrance to the garage. "Thank you all for coming today." He pumps my dad's hand, then mine, and saves a hug for Pockets. We all come away wiping grease off various body parts. It's funny how when I first met Graff all I could think about was that he looked like a giant ant. Now he just looks like Graff.

"I know what a special occasion it is

when your son joins forces with you," Dad says, winking at me. "We wouldn't miss it."

Graff grins and ruffles my hair. Good thing my dark hair hides the grease that just squirted out of Graff's hand!

"Hello, Feemus," Graff says with a nod. "Always nice to see you."

"You know Feemus?" I ask.

"Of course," Graff says. "Everyone knows the head of Pockets' fan club. Where Pockets goes, Feemus is never far behind." Pockets hisses in response to that comment. Graff puts one arm around Pockets' shoulders and the other around mine. "Come on, boys, let me introduce you to my son, Kurf."

Graff leads us over to a silver car/spaceship with legs sticking out from underneath. Graff bends down, grabs the ankles, and gently pulls. Out slides a boy who looks identical to Graff, only a few decades younger. "Hi, Pops!" the boy says. "Is this him?" He gestures to me.

"Me?" I ask, surprised.

Graff nods. "I figured you and Kurf are around the same age. You'd probably like a buddy to hang out with while you're here."

I glance over to Dad and Pockets. Dad gives me a nod.

"Sure!" I reply. Kurf waves to me, which is definitely better than a handshake if he's anything like his dad! Judging by the puddle of oil he's standing in, he'd get me messy pretty quickly. I wave back.

Feemus clears his throat. "I don't mean to break up the start of a lovely friendship, but we've got to move this ceremony along."

"Here ya go," Pockets says, tossing a

gold-colored wrench at Kurf. Tools to them are apparently like trophies to Earth kids. Kurf catches it inches away from his head.

"Congratulations," Pockets adds.

"Thanks!" Kurf says, holding it up for everyone to see. Graff cheers loudest.

Feemus groans. "There was supposed to be a whole thing here. Speeches, standing ovations, ribbon cutting."

"That's okay," Kurf says. "Hey, can Archie hang out for a while? I can show him around."

"I'm afraid that won't be possible," Feemus says, whipping out the itinerary. "Our schedule is totally full. We have lunch next with some very important world leaders."

"What if Kurf comes along with us?" Dad suggests. He turns to Graff. "Would that be okay? Pockets and I will keep an eye on him."

Pockets shakes his head.

"*I* will keep an eye on him," Dad corrects himself.

"Sure," Graff says. "Would you like to, son?"

Kurf has already pulled off his mechanic's overalls and tossed on a baseball cap. "Let's go!"

Chapter Five:
Slog-Eating Contest

What I take away from the lunch is that important leaders are really serious and only want to talk about politics and security and grown-up stuff. Pockets is still annoyed at the lack of tuna and is being very vocal about it to anyone who will listen.

The leaders keep asking his opinions on important matters, and Pockets looks like he wants to crawl under the table.

Kurf and I really DO crawl under the table, until Dad makes us come out. Then we spend the rest of the time daring each other to try the really weird foods the waiters keep serving. I swear, some of it is still moving! I'm not a picky eater (only room for one of those in the family, and Penny's already gotten dibs on that) but eating tiny black slugs or some kind of furry meat with feathers still on it just doesn't do it for me. Kurf wins our contest hands down. He even eats a napkin! I, on the other hand, leave lunch hungry.

Then it's back to the tailors' to try on our new suits. I thought wearing a suit would feel all itchy and tight, but mine fits great! I look like I stepped out of a clothing catalog! I admire it from all angles while Kurf nods approvingly. "You clean up good!" he says. "For a human."

I grin.

"What about me?" Dad asks, holding his arms out wide.

"Two thumbs-up," I tell him. "If you wear that home, Mom'll think I left my real dad up here at Akbar's!"

"Two pounds!" the tailor shrieks as he circles around Pockets. "How could you gain *two pounds* in one meal?"

"If I'd had *tuna* to eat, I wouldn't have had to stuff myself with bread!" Pockets throws up his paws. As he does, his suit rips right down the seams.

Feemus looks ready to faint from embarrassment. "Take it off," the tailor cries. "I'll have to start all over!"

It takes so long to remake the suit that we miss the tour of the gardens. I think it's safe to say that no one (except maybe Feemus) is too broken up about that. Kurf checks out the itinerary and says, "Yay! We get to go to the slog-eating contest! That's been sold out for weeks!"

"What's a slog, anyway?" I ask.

"Ohhh, you're gonna love it! Just make sure you don't sit in the front row!"

So, of course, where are our seats? That's right: row one, front and center! We're apparently considered "special guests," since Pockets is the judge. The fact that there are rain ponchos on each seat is a bit worrisome. A long table has been set up in the front of the room, with six giant bowls across from six folding chairs. As the judge, Pockets will be standing behind the contestants to make sure they're actually eating the food and not hiding it in their laps.

One by one, the contestants file in to thunderous applause and take their seats on the stage.

"Bloppy!" I shout as the last contestant enters. I'd recognize my big goopy friend anywhere! Who else looks like a melting orange snowman? I jump out of my chair. "Dad, it's Bloppy!"

"I can see that," Dad says, clapping louder.

"Bloppy is the favorite to win," Kurf

explains. "He may have a small mouth, but he chews faster than anyone. In fact, I'm not sure he even chews; he may just shovel it in!"

As Bloppy glides to the front of the room, goo oozes off him and then slurps back up onto his body, as usual. A strange condition of his species, but that's what makes him so perfect for his job at Akbar's roller rink: keeping the floors clean and smooth. "Archie! Sal!" he calls out when he sees us in the audience. "Thanks so much for coming!" We cheer some more and wave.

"Pockets!" Bloppy shouts as he gets to the stage. He reaches for a hug, but Pockets holds up his paw to stop him. Pockets is not a hugger. Plus, it probably wouldn't look good for the judge of the contest to hug a contestant!

Once the contestants are all seated, waiters enter carrying huge white buckets. Pockets makes sure an even amount gets poured into each bowl. "Ick!" I whisper to Kurf. "The slog looks like chunks of rotten garbage!"

"That's exactly what it is!" Kurf says, laughing.

A foul smell rises up from the bowls, and I have to cover my nose. I'm pretty sure my first slog-eating contest will also be my last. Pockets blows a whistle and the contestants begin shoveling the slog into their mouths. "Quick!" Kurf shouts. "Put on your poncho!"

The audience cheers as slog goes flying out of the bowls in all directions. Pockets is protecting himself by erecting a force field

in front of himself. I yank the hood farther down over my face and peek out. Bloppy's doing great, but the guy next to him in a green-striped suit has almost emptied his bowl! The card in front of his seat says his name is Thoster. He has a wide mouth that extends almost all the way across his even wider face. He reminds me of a capital *T*— a wide head and a skinny body. I'll never get tired of seeing new kinds of aliens.

Right as I'm sure Bloppy's about to lose, Thoster glances over at him. He then stops eating to pick his teeth with his pinkie nail! The crowd's going nuts! Bloppy slurps up the last of the slog and Pockets blows the whistle. "Bloppy is the winner," Pockets announces, looking bored and slightly annoyed. "I should be saving the universe right now," he mutters loud enough for me to hear. "Instead I'm doing *this*?"

Feemus jumps up and runs to the table. I figure he's going to congratulate Bloppy, but instead he gets right up in Thoster's face. "Throwing the contest?" Feemus shouts at him. "That's...that's...well, it's not cool!"

"Feemus!" Dad says, jumping up. "Leave the man alone. You don't know that he let Bloppy win!"

"That's okay, sir," Thoster says. "I *did* let him win. He deserved it. He has a very small mouth, and I have a very large one."

Feemus shakes his head. "That may be. But you let Bloppy win because you know he's Pockets' friend and you want Pockets to like you."

"Wait," Dad says, "what's going on with you two?"

Feemus glares at Thoster, who is wiping off his hand before holding it out to Dad. "I'm Thoster. I joined Pockets' fan club a few weeks ago, and the little guy feels threatened by me." He pats Feemus on the head. "But truly, there is no reason. There's enough of Pockets to go around."

At the sound of his name, Pockets jumps. Thoster turns to look adoringly up at him. Dad and I have to hide our laughs behind our hands. Feemus seems to have met his match! Guess he's not the only member of the fan club after all!

Pockets lowers himself onto his four paws and scampers through the crowd until he's at the door. Feemus shakes his head at Thoster one more time and runs after Pockets. I want to go talk to Bloppy, but he's having his picture taken with his medal.

Unfortunately, Kurf has to go home before the rehearsal dinner, so we say our good-byes covered in slog. "Have fun in your fancy hotel room," Kurf teases.

"I will!" I reply, although we've barely been in there long enough for me to remember what it looks like.

Dad and I stop at one of the restrooms on the way to the ballroom to clean up from the contest. Getting the smell out of my nose is something that soap and water isn't going to fix!

It's a little past six when Dad and I arrive at dinner. My lack of sleep is starting to catch up to me again. I yawn as I look around the enormous ballroom. Pockets and his father are in deep conversation in the corner. The last time I saw them together, they were acting like typical cats—rolling around on the floor and leaping around each other. Guess this isn't exactly the right occasion for being silly. Assorted aliens clutching autograph books and cameras look on in adoration. These could only be the fan club members. I spot Thoster and wave. He tips his hat at me. A small chunk of slog hangs from his ear. I shudder as he pulls it off and pops it into his mouth.

The chief abruptly turns to face the room. "All right, everyone. Let's get this show on the road." He gives orders to the waitstaff, telling them which guests will be at which tables tomorrow and to make sure everyone has at least one tuna sandwich before offering seconds. He turns to the stage, where Feemus is fiddling with the microphone. "A short film of Pockets will play in the background while the guests are getting settled and eating their salads and soup. Then Feemus will make his opening remarks."

At the sound of his name, Feemus drops the microphone and a loud squeak shoots from the speakers. "Sorry, sorry!" he says, quickly grabbing it. "It's an honor to meet you in the flesh, sir, truly, just the biggest thrill." He makes an awkward bowing motion.

The chief takes a deep breath and continues. "After the remarks, I shall come up to present my son with the award." He turns to Pockets. "Then it will be your turn to give your speech. Do you want to practice now?"

Pockets' ears press down against his head. "No!" he says. "I mean, wouldn't it mean more to hear it for the first time at the ceremony?"

The chief nods and pats his son on the head. "Good thinking."

Dad and I exchange a look. Pockets just got off easy. I'd be surprised if he's written even one sentence of that speech so far.

The chief seems satisfied that everything will go smoothly, so we sit down to eat. The main course is some kind of stew, and even though it's bright green, it doesn't look as bad as what they served for lunch.

Dad digs right in. Unfortunately, the stink from the slog is still in my nose, so even if dinner were pizza or hot dogs, I don't think I'd be able to eat. I don't drink much, either. The kitchen ran out of ice, so all the drinks are warm and not refreshing at all.

Apparently I fell asleep at the table, because the next thing I know I'm in my bed and Dad is turning out the light.

Chapter Six:
What, No Tuna?!?!

"Good morning, young Morningstar," a voice sings in my ear. "Time to wake up. You have a big day ahead of you."

"Mom?" I ask groggily. "Penny?"

A voice like a tinkling bell laughs. "No, dear, I am your alarm clock."

"Huh?" I open my eyes. A glowing yellow ball is floating about a foot above my bed. I rub my eyes. It's still there!

"I see that you are awake," the voice says.

It's coming from the ball!

"I shall turn myself off now," the ball says. "Have a lovely day." The ball gracefully glides back to the night table, settles down with a nearly soundless *plop*, and stops glowing. As I reach for it, my door opens and Dad walks in, holding his own yellow ball. We both start laughing. "This is definitely a better way to wake up than Penny pulling open my eyelids!" he says.

"At least I'm not the only one she does that to," I joke.

"I'm glad *someone's* having fun," a gloomy voice says.

"Pockets?" I sit up. He's lying curled up at the bottom of the huge bed. I didn't even feel him there. "Did you sleep here all night? You have your own bedroom, you know."

"I just want to get back to work," he complains. "I don't even know what the team has found on the *Galactic* recently. They may have uncovered some data that will unravel B.U.R.P. for good. And what am I doing? Judging slog contests and eating too much bread."

"Remember your new motto about getting into it?"

Pockets just grunts and buries his head.

"Everyone up?" Feemus' voice echoes through the large suite.

"If I say no, will you leave?" Pockets calls from under his paw.

Feemus races into the room. "I have your clothes." He holds up three long suit bags and hands one to each of us. Pockets grabs his and goes into the bathroom to put it on, muttering the whole time.

Room service has delivered a delicious breakfast of normal human pancakes, which is a good thing, because I'm so hungry. I wish I'd waited to put my suit on, though. Hopefully no one will notice the line of syrup down my sleeve!

Dad and I walk into the ballroom later feeling pretty good about ourselves. We're well fed, all dressed up in our spiffy new suits, and ready to have fun. Pockets, on the other hand, is none of those things. He didn't eat a bite of breakfast, so his suit is now too loose and his head keeps slipping down into the neck hole. Also, he left a trail of crumpled notebook pages between our hotel room and here.

The only one more anxious than Pockets right now is Feemus. He's dashing around chairs and under tables, making sure everything is exactly how he wants it. He's adjusting lights, fluffing flower

arrangements, and tapping the microphone over and over. The room is filling up with all sorts of well-dressed aliens, many wearing ISF badges, from all over the universe. The largest group by far, though, is the ISF cats from Friskopolus.

"Hey!" I shout, pointing across at a cat animatedly telling a story to a bunch of other cats. "Isn't that Hector? From planet Tri-Dark?"

"I never met him," Dad says. "Remember? I was working to fix the taxi for the whole mission. You go say hi. I'm going to see if I can help Pockets finish that speech."

I run toward the crowd of ISF cats. "Hector!" I shout. "It's me, Archie. I'm wearing a suit!"

"Archie!" he cries, thrusting out his

paw for me to shake it. "I was just talking about you!"

"You *were*?"

He nods. "I was telling these fellas about how you and Pockets saved Princess Viola. Also that little red dude who's running around here like his behind is on fire."

I laugh. "Feemus is definitely a little more nervous than usual today. So, how's the princess?"

"Great," he says. "She just beat three princes and a knight in a jousting tournament, then beat all of them at a belching contest."

"Sounds like her!"

"Yup."

I want to ask if she remembers me, but I know she doesn't. That was part of what we had to give up in order to save her.

A screech echoes through the speakers and everyone cringes. "Sorry," Feemus says. "If you'll all take your seats, we can get started. I know you're as anxious as I am to hear from the guest of honor! Please enjoy this film as your salads are being served."

"Great seeing you, Archie," Hector says as he heads off to a table in the front. "Let's catch up later."

As I turn to find my own table, some yelling and banging from the kitchen catch my attention. I watch as three of the security guards hired by Akbar's for the event slip into the kitchen. "Come on, Archie," Dad says, pulling me away. "I'm sure we don't want to miss a second of this!"

We take our seats across from Pockets' dad. A seat is empty for Akbar, but so far there's no sign of him. I'm not sure anyone even knows what he looks like! The lights dim and a screen lowers behind the podium. Pockets as a kitten chasing an electric mouse up a wall fills the screen. Everyone cheers and laughs. He is SOOOOOO cute!!! Penny would LOSE HER MIND. I lean over to Dad. "We've GOT to get a copy of this!"

"Already got that covered," he replies, holding his phone up to the screen.

Pockets reddens and slides his head down through the neck hole of his suit. The waiters begin wheeling around carts with

salads on them, but everyone is enjoying the film too much to eat. We watch Pockets grow from a kitten to a cat, and even get to see him solving his first crime. His father chuckles and says, "My wife filmed that from behind a bush!"

More and more clips of him solving crimes play on the screen. Agents begin to murmur among themselves. Who was taking all these videos? Then a clip flies by of Pockets in a space taxi. OUR space taxi!! Dad and I look at each other, agape. Then we turn to look at the only one who could have filmed all this. Feemus! He gets AROUND!

Feemus beams as he watches the video, his antennae swishing happily. When the video ends, the audience stands to applaud.

Feemus is practically shaking with excitement as he returns to the microphone. "So as you can all see, our beloved Pilarbing Fangorious—now known as Pockets—has been achieving great things for many years. Now, I know you didn't come to hear *me* talk, so—"

"That's right! We came for Barney's tuna sandwiches!" a member of a rowdy group of ISF cats shouts out.

Everybody laughs. Feemus wobbles a little bit at the outburst but quickly recovers. "I'm sure you don't want those as badly as Pockets does! I've seen him eat a whole tray at once!"

The audience laughs.

"I will now call the chief ISF officer from Friskopolus to the stage, where he will present his son with this most rare and special award." Pockets' father stands up, straightens his tie, and heads toward Pockets. At the same time, four of Akbar's security guards storm the stage. At first I assume they're part of the show. But they pass right by the chief and approach Feemus, who is still holding out the mic to Pockets' dad.

The guards surround Feemus, who looks stunned. "You will have to come with us," one of them says. "Right now."

"Is this a joke?" Feemus asks. He cranes his neck around to see into the crowd. "Pockets, did you put them up to this? I'm actually quite touched, but I know everyone's probably hungry, so..."

Pockets pokes his head back out of his

suit and jumps up when he sees all the action on the stage. "What's going on?"

"Unhand Feemus at once!" the chief demands.

"I'm sorry, sir," one of the guards says, "but he is under arrest for theft. We have it on film."

"I didn't steal anything," Feemus insists. "You have the wrong guy."

Pockets' whole fan club calls out, "He would never ruin Pockets' big day! He's innocent!"

"I don't think so," the guard says. Then he points a remote control at the screen and a video begins to play.

Security camera footage first shows an empty corridor. Then a large cart appears, like the kind the waiters are pushing with salads. Only this one is full of tuna fish sandwiches! A gasp rises from the crowd as Feemus appears in the frame, pushing the cart straight out of the kitchen!

The video is blurry and it keeps flickering, making Feemus look like he's walking stiffly and a little awkwardly. The color isn't great, either. Feemus looks more orange than red at times. The video cuts out for a second, then flickers back on to reveal Feemus wheeling the cart toward the front door of his ship. Right before he enters, he turns, spots the video camera, and—amazingly—smiles! The video freezes up, right there on his guilty face.

The lights in the ballroom blaze on as the crowd jumps to their feet. The ISF cats rush the stage, shouting, "You stole the *tuna*?"

Pockets does a front handspring over the ISF cats' heads and lands on the stage. His face is more expressive than it's been since we got here—ears pointed straight up, eyes wide and focused. I can tell a part of him is furious about the tuna, but that part is overpowered by his happiness at being back in the crime-solving business. "Feemus!" he demands. "Can you explain yourself?"

Feemus only stares at the image of himself on the screen in stunned silence. He shakes his head.

"Where's the tuna now?" one of the guests shouts.

"Feemus' ship is no longer docked at

Akbar's," the guard says. "Therefore, we were unable to recover the sandwiches." The crowd begins to boo. Dad pulls me close.

The guard holds up his hand and the room quiets down. "We are sorry to interrupt your lunch. We will escort the criminal to the security office and take care of it from there."

"I'm coming, too," Pockets says.

"Wait!" the chief shouts.

Pockets stops. His father walks up to him and lays a medal around his neck. "For your courage on planet Canis, honesty, intelligence, and the capture of the *Galactic*. I'm proud of you, son."

Pockets lifts the medal with one paw, then lets it fall back against his chest.

"Thank you, Father," he says. "Now I've got to go do my job."

Using one sharp claw, he slices through the front of his suit. It drops to the floor at his feet. With a forward double somersault that I'm not sure is entirely necessary, he rolls off the stage and joins the guards leading Feemus down the aisle.

The crowd parts to let them through. When Feemus reaches me and Dad, he looks up, eye shiny. I think he's about to start crying, and I don't blame him. He's gotten himself in a real pickle. But then he smiles and says, "Pockets is going to investigate me! *Me!* How exciting is *that*?"

Chapter Seven:
The New Guy

Dad and I get to the security office in time to hear Pockets say, "I know why you did it. I'm flattered and all, but this is a serious crime."

"I didn't do it," Feemus insists, but he can't seem to wipe the smile from his face, so his argument isn't very convincing.

"You knew how much I wanted that tuna," Pockets says, whipping out a recording device, "so you tried to take it all for me. In the end, it wasn't the best idea. Let's just admit that, bring back your odd little round spaceship, and return the tuna to the kitchen. I'm sure all those tuna-starved ISF cats will forgive you if you feed them."

"I would if I could," Feemus says. "But I didn't take it. And I don't know where my ship is."

Pockets throws up his paws. "Then why are you smiling?"

"I'm sorry!" Feemus says. "It's just that the great Pilarbing Fangorious is interrogating me. It's exciting!"

"Trust me," one of Akbar's security guards says, "you won't find jail all that exciting, and that's where you're headed."

"Look, Feemus," Pockets says, and I can tell he feels a little sorry for him. "This isn't a game. I saw that video. We all saw it."

"But that wasn't me," Feemus insists. "I was with you guys all the time. Well, I guess not *all* the time, since sometimes you ditched me, but most of the time!"

Dad and I exchange a guilty look. It probably wasn't nice to ditch him, but he can be a little exhausting. "Are you denying that was you on the video?" Dad asks.

"Yes," Feemus says firmly. The Akbar security guards shake their heads at that. They aren't buying it.

"Could you have done it in your sleep?" I ask. "Have you ever sleepwalked before?"

"I don't think so," Feemus says. His smile wobbles. "The worst part of this? I could lose my position as president of the fan club! The other members will argue that I'm not fit to stand by your side."

"*That's* the worst part?" Pockets asks. "That someone else might be the president of my..." He can't make himself say the words *fan club*.

Feemus nods, his thin shoulders sagging. "Someone else will become your right-hand man. The person you rely on most, the one who knows your fears, your dreams, who can figure out your needs before you even have them." He wipes away a tear.

Pockets stares at Feemus and shakes his head. "You've really got to get another hobby."

One of the guards comes in. "Feemus has a visitor."

Thoster pushes his way through. "I came as soon as I could."

"I guess you're here on official president business," Feemus says glumly.

Thoster nods. "It's only a temporary position, don't worry. Pockets needs someone by his side in this time of crisis."

"No, I don't," Pockets says, shaking his head emphatically.

"No," Feemus says sadly. "Thoster's right. You definitely need a sidekick."

"Ahem," I say. "I'm pretty sure my dad and I are his sidekicks?"

Feemus and Thoster roll their eyes. Well, Feemus only rolls the one. Still, I don't appreciate it. We make excellent sidekicks!

"There you guys are!" a voice says from behind us. I turn around to find Kurf. "Been looking all over for you."

"You found us!" I say, happy to see him.

"Feemus' ship showed up!" he says, turning to Pockets. "My dad found it hidden under a blanket behind a broken transport bot."

"Good!" Pockets declares, heading toward the door. "The tuna has been found and we can put this whole unfortunate affair behind us." Then he glares at Feemus and says, "After a written apology."

Feemus begins to follow Pockets out the door, but the security guards block him. "You'll need to stay here until this is sorted out."

With a longing glance at Pockets, Feemus allows himself to be led back in. "Don't worry," Thoster says. "I will keep Pockets company and make sure his needs are taken care of."

Feemus sinks down onto the bench. I feel sorry for him, even though he brought this upon himself. Or did he?

Apparently the transport bots are only allowed to be in the hotel, so we'll have to walk nearly the whole length of the rest stop to get to Graff's Garage. As I do my best to keep up, I run the facts of the case through my head like Pockets taught me. Since Feemus ALWAYS wants Pockets to be happy, it's logical that he would have stolen the tuna. But if he did, then why not give it to Pockets sooner? Why wait until the lunch? Did he steal it just to gain Pockets' attention? If so, then why bother to deny that he stole it in the first place? Nothing adds up.

I would go over it with Pockets, but

Thoster is busy asking him lots of questions, like any good fan club member would do if they got the chance to walk alongside their idol. *How did you stand it, being so close to all those wild dogs? What did it feel like to capture the* Galactic*? Has the ISF found any good information on board? What's your favorite pizza topping? Do you think B.U.R.P. will be a threat again anytime soon?*

Pockets only gives one-word answers. Mostly he just grunts. He's a cat on a mission, and right now that mission includes retrieving a tray of tuna fish sandwiches. No one can compete with that.

"Careful," Kurf says, pointing to a puddle of water that I never would have noticed. "When your body squirts oil, you learn to avoid water," he explains. "Oil and water don't mix!"

I look past the puddle and see a trail of water leading down an alley between shops. I'm surprised, because Akbar's is always very clean. Someone could slip on that. Thoster must be thinking the same thing, because he stops and stares down at it. "Pockets always has towels in one of his pockets," I tell him. "I'll go get one."

"No need to slow him down," Thoster says. He points to a closet nearby marked JANITORIAL SUPPLIES. "I'll take care of it." A few seconds later the spill has a plastic orange cone next to it, warning, CAUTION, WET FLOOR.

"Smart!" I say.

Pockets is so focused on the tuna that

he keeps bumping into people. At one point he almost bumps into a guy carrying two huge buckets of ice—I think it's that same blue guy I've seen twice now! He's either a really big fan of ice or it's his job to deliver it. Thoster quickly jumps between Pockets and the ice guy. Thoster makes sure to shield Pockets with his body until the guy heads off, an ice cube flying out from his buckets now and then. "Phew!" he says, mopping his brow. "That was a close one. Pockets might have gotten hurt. Or very wet!" He is clearly taking his self-appointed duties as president very seriously. Feemus would be pleased. Jealous, but pleased.

When we finally get to Graff's Garage to retrieve the tuna, it turns out Feemus' ship is totally empty. "Did someone take the sandwiches to the ballroom already?" Dad asks.

Before Graff can answer, Pockets shakes his head. "There has never been any tuna on board this spaceship."

CHAPTER EIGHT:
Roller Rink Revenge

"How is that possible?" one of the guards asks. "We all saw the footage. He was pushing those sandwiches right through this very door."

"Maybe he dropped them off someplace and cleaned out his ship," Thoster suggests.

Pockets shakes his head. "If there had been any tuna here in the last twenty-four hours, I would still smell it." I can tell by the slow way he's talking and the downward tilt of his ears that he's only barely keeping it together.

Thoster tries again. "Could he have moved the sandwiches to your space taxi so you could eat them on your ride home?"

Pockets shakes his head again. "The security cameras in the hotel parking garage would have picked up his movements."

"Poor little guy," Thoster says. "He made a bad choice, but he did it out of affection. I guess they'll have to hold him here on Akbar's until they can find the missing sandwiches."

While the others are trying to figure out where the tuna is, I take the opportunity to peek inside. Feemus' ship is basically the shape of a cupcake, and not much taller than me! Like our space taxi, though, I've seen Feemus' ship hold a lot more inside than it would appear from the outside.

The dashboard doesn't look anything like the one in Dad's taxi. There are a lot more buttons and knobs and levers. Obviously his spaceship can do a lot more than our taxi can. I guess it would have to, the way Feemus manages to get places so quickly.

I feel a little strange looking around, like I'm invading his private space. I realize I don't know much about him—how old he is, how he met Pockets, where he lives. On the back of his seat he taped a photo of him and Pockets holding a captured B.U.R.P. criminal between them. Feemus is smiling wide and Pockets is scowling. There's another picture with Feemus on a boat with three other little red aliens who could only be his family. I kneel down to peer a little closer at it. I wonder if he sees his family often. I wonder if they're as obsessed with Pockets as he is.

When I climb back out, Kurf points to my knees and says, "You got something on your nice suit." I look down to see a smudge of what looks like orange paint on each knee.

"What is that?" Dad asks, coming closer.

"Let me help," Thoster says, and he licks it off! I guess I shouldn't be so surprised. This is the guy who ate a huge bowl of garbage yesterday. But still, it's kind of a strange thing to do.

"Let's get back to Feemus," Pockets says. "I didn't want to have to resort to it, but I can use the Truth or Lie 2000 on him. Then we can finish this thing."

The whole way back, Thoster divides his time between clearing a path for Pockets and peppering him with questions again. *What was your hardest mission? What are your favorite gadgets? How does someone become an ISF officer?* Finally, Pockets just slips on a pair of headphones and Thoster stops asking.

"Hey, the cone is gone," I point out as we reach the spill.

Pockets stops and pulls off his headphones. "What did you say?" he asks.

"Nothing, really," I reply. "Just that there's some water on the floor. We had a cone there to warn people, but it's gone."

"There it is," Dad says, pointing a few yards away, to the entrance of the Fresh As a Daisy flower shop. It must have gotten kicked there by mistake.

"Keep moving," Thoster says, steering Pockets away while Dad goes to get the cone. But Pockets does not like to be steered. He looks down to see what I was talking about.

"Strange," he murmurs. "It leads into a closet, not a restroom. Why would a closet be leaking water?" He starts walking toward it, but Thoster reaches it first and tries to turn the knob.

"It's locked," he says. "We should go

back to Feemus anyway. Probably just a janitor's bucket leaking."

Thoster obviously doesn't realize that Pockets can't turn away from a mystery, even one as small as why a closet is leaking water.

"You're just turning the knob the wrong way," Pockets says. He slips in front of Thoster and pushes open the door. It's cold in the closet, and dark. Pockets flicks on the light, and the first thing I see is that bumpy blue guy! He looks as surprised to see us as we are to see him. He lunges across the small space, like he's trying to cover something up. Then I see it. A huge cart full of ice. No wonder the kitchen was out of ice—it was all in here! And on top of the ice? About a hundred tuna fish sandwiches! He must have needed the ice so the sandwiches wouldn't go bad!

"Why'd you bring them here, boss?" asks Blue Guy.

No one says anything, not sure if they misheard the guy. "Sorry, what?" Pockets says. "Are you working with Feemus?"

"Huh?" Blue Guy says. It's at this point that I notice Thoster is slowly backing out of the closet. Pockets notices, too. In a flash, he's on top of him.

"What's going on, Thoster?" he demands. "If that is even your name."

I look from Blue Guy to Thoster and back again. Blue Guy looks confused. Thoster's eyes are black with fury. Dad pulls me away. I'm very confused. Has Thoster been working with Feemus all this time? Or did he steal the sandwiches and frame Feemus so he could become president of the fan club? It certainly looks that way. But how did he get Feemus in that video?

"It was Feemus' idea!" Thoster insists. "He just wanted to please you. All I did was promise to keep his secret."

Pockets loosens his grip a tiny bit. It just doesn't sound right to me, though. Feemus never trusted Thoster to begin with. I think back to the little I know about Thoster. All this time I thought he was being nice—first to Bloppy at the contest, then to Pockets—but he was just trying to get on Pockets' good side and earn his trust, just like Feemus said. And just before, in the hallway, he wasn't trying to save Blue Guy from spilling ice on Pockets—he was trying to keep Pockets from spotting him and getting suspicious. Even putting out the cone wasn't about keeping people from slipping; it was about making sure Pockets stayed clear of the water so he wouldn't trace it back to the closet! Or maybe I'm wrong—after all, Thoster *did* clean the paint off my pants for me. Then, suddenly, I realize why he did it.

"Wait!" I shout to Pockets, who has started to help Thoster to his feet. "He's lying. The orange paint! That wasn't Feemus in that video at all!" I turn to Pockets. "Now I know why Feemus was walking all weird and looked orange instead of red."

"That's absurd," Thoster says.

I race around the closet, looking for anything to help prove my story, like a jar of paint. Then I spot something orange sticking out from underneath the cart with the ice. As I dive down to the floor, Blue Guy grabs at my suit collar.

"Unhand him," Pockets growls. His tail swishes around and unhinges, and a laser shoots out and nips Blue Guy's ear. He howls and lets me go. I yank out the orange thing and find myself holding one very odd-looking Feemus-shaped robot.

"Who ARE you?" Pockets demands. "Nobody goes to all this trouble just to become the president of my fan club!" He pulls out his tablet and holds it up to Thoster's face. Thoster grunts and tries to break free. A few seconds later the tablet dings and a photo comes up on the screen. *Warning: B.U.R.P. officer. Wanted for theft on sixteen planets. Considered armed and dangerous. Current assignment: Spy. Mission: Find and befriend Pockets the cat in order to find out his secrets.*

Dad, Kurf, and I gasp. We don't have too much time to react, though, because things move fast! Thoster takes advantage of the fact that Pockets is only holding him with one paw. He reaches into his boot and pulls out some kind of device the size of a television remote control. Before Pockets can grab it, Thoster pushes a button. Instantly, we—and everything around us that's not nailed down—float about six feet off the ground!

"We're flying!" Kurf shouts. He stretches out his arms and soars higher toward the ceiling.

I laugh. This is awesome! Even Pockets is floating. Hissing and spitting, but floating. A tuna sandwich floats right up to his nose. He gobbles it down in one bite. Dad holds on to a high shelf and points down at the floor. It takes a few seconds before I realize that Thoster is still standing upright.

"Gravity boots," he says, grinning with that wide mouth of his. He gives us a wave and then darts right out of the storage room.

Pockets scowls. "He's good, I'll give him that. But he's not getting off this rest stop." He taps his ear communicator and contacts Akbar's security team. "Lock down the docking bays until further notice. No one takes off." To the rest of us he says, "The anti-gravity must only work in here. We'd know if the rest of Akbar's was on the ceiling!"

We half glide, half swim out of the storage room and instantly fall to the ground. Pockets scrambles to his feet and throws a net over Blue Guy, who made the mistake of following us out. Pockets radios security again to come get the criminal and to bring nets to rescue the floating sandwiches.

Kurf and I stare up at the high ceiling of the rest stop, catching our breath. Kurf turns to me. "Does stuff like this happen to you a lot?"

I nod. "More than you'd think."

"I'm so glad I met you!" Kurf says, holding up his hand. I give him an enthusiastic high five. This suit is pretty much ruined by now, so what's a little oil?

I follow Pockets' gaze as he looks down the hall in both directions. One way is crowded with aliens going about their business. If Thoster had run through the crowd, people would be stopped and looking around, or knocked over. The other way is the roller rink, which is closed now for the day. I'm about to point out my observations to Pockets, but he's already on his feet.

"C'mon," he says to the rest of us. "He's probably hiding out at the rink." I smile. I'm getting better at this detective stuff!

We race down to the rink. "He wouldn't have had much time to hide," Pockets notes, "so he should be pretty easy to spot."

And sure enough, when we get there we see the back of Thoster's head sticking out from behind the skate rental booth. The only other person in the rink is Bloppy, who is standing beside his locker on the other side of the rink.

"Freeze!" Pockets shouts. But Thoster does the opposite. He takes off across the rink, heading for the back exit door.

"Quick, Bloppy!" Pockets shouts. "Do your thing!"

Bloppy turns and looks from Pockets to Thoster. At first I can see his confusion. After all, this is the guy who let him win the contest.

"He's a B.U.R.P. agent," I shout. "And he's getting away!"

Bloppy quickly glides onto the rink, letting loose a steady stream of goop as he goes. Thoster runs right into it! His boots fly up in the air and he lands square on his back with a loud "Oomph!" He tries to scramble to his feet but just keeps slipping and falling. Kurf and I have to put our hands over our mouths to keep from laughing. Bloppy circles around him, keeping him trapped.

A little while later, after Thoster is safely in ISF custody, a small group of us gathers back in the ballroom—a freed Feemus, Bloppy, Hector, Dad, me, Graff and Kurf, and Pockets and his dad.

"Before we all go our separate ways," Pockets says, clutching something in his paw, "I figured out why I struggled to write my acceptance speech. It was because it wasn't MY award to accept in the first place. Yes, I did go to planet Canis, but the mission was truly a team effort, and as proven again today, I have the best team." He pauses and looks over at me and Dad, and then at Bloppy, who beams happily.

"Some of the people who support me couldn't be here today, but we know they're thinking of us." Pockets opens his paw now to reveal the plastic four-leaf clover Penny gave him! "So it is on their behalf," he continues, "and for the brave ISF agents who stormed the spaceship *Galactic* with me and who are now escorting the criminal Thoster and his henchman back to Friskopolus, that I accept this award."

Pockets' dad thumps him on the back. The rest of us wipe away tears while trying to pretend we have something in our eyes. Bloppy, however, is a slobbering mess. No one cries like Bloppy.

"Hey, Feemus," I ask, "did you happen to get that speech on film?"

"Of course," he says. "What kind of fan club president would I be if I hadn't?"

"Can you save a copy for me?" I ask.

"There's someone I want to show it to when she's a little older."

"Certainly," Feemus says. "Hey, wasn't it spectacular how Pockets figured out the whole tuna thing? He's so amazing. Just brilliant how he puts all the clues together!"

I blink. It's like Feemus didn't even hear what Pockets just said about crime-solving being a team effort.

But Feemus isn't done. "And Pockets should get another award for freeing me and capturing the B.U.R.P. agent," he says. "All single-handedly!"

I sigh and walk away. Some things will never change.

And you know what? I wouldn't want them to.

THREE SCIENCE FACTS TO IMPRESS YOUR FRIENDS AND TEACHERS

1. The path an object takes in space as it travels around another object is called its ORBIT. The mass of the larger object keeps the smaller one from flying away. For example, the moon orbits Earth, while the planets in our solar system orbit the sun. Akbar's Floating Rest Stop orbits the whole Milky Way galaxy! We have put all sorts of cool things into orbit around Earth, including satellites to track weather patterns and for communication, telescopes to take pictures of deep space, and one of humanity's greatest achievements, the International Space Station, where astronauts and scientists can live for months at a time in order to conduct experiments in space.

2. The INTERNATIONAL SPACE STATION (ISS for short) floats in orbit 220 miles from Earth. It may not be as big as Akbar's Floating Rest Stop, but it's as large as a professional soccer field and weighs almost 400 tons! Each time a part needs to be added, it has to be built on Earth and launched into space, and astronauts have to attach it. The ISS is a truly international venture, with scientists from the United States, Canada, Japan, the

European Union, and Russia contributing to it and performing experiments that will help all of mankind.

3. Whenever Archie meets a new alien, he marvels at how different each species can be. This is also true on Earth, where there are so many different habitats (places where animals can live) that creatures have adapted the traits necessary to survive in that area. Scientists call this **BiODiVERSitY**. There is more biodiversity in the warmer parts of Earth than in the colder ones. So far scientists have found 1.7 million different species on Earth, and they estimate there may be as many as 50 million more! It's important for humans to protect our planet's biodiversity.

Elise Gravel

WENDY MASS has written lots of books for kids, including *The Candymakers*, a *New York Times* bestseller; *Every Soul a Star*; and *Pi in the Sky*. MICHAEL BRAWER is a teacher who drives space taxis on the side. They live in New Jersey with their two kids and two cats, none of whom have left the solar system.

GET READY TO GO INTERGALACTIC!

SPACE TAXI B.U.R.P. STRIKES BACK

SPACE TAXI ARCHIE'S ALIEN DISGUISE

SPACE TAXI THE GALACTIC B.U.R.P.

SPACE TAXI WATER PLANET RESCUE

SPACE TAXI ARCHIE TAKES FLIGHT

WENDY MASS AND MICHAEL BRAWER

The out-of-this-world series by
WENDY MASS
and
MICHAEL BRAWER

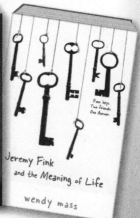